ALEXANDER

by Harold Littledale · illustrated by Tom Vroman

Parents' Magazine Press
A Division of Parents' Magazine Enterprises, Inc.
52 Vanderbilt Ave., New York, N. Y. 10017

It was bedtime. Chris and his father sat side by side on Chris's bed.

"Alexander was a pretty bad horse today," Chris said.

His father lit his pipe. "Alexander, the red horse with green stripes?"

Chris nodded.

"What happened?" Chris's father asked.

"He wouldn't eat his cereal,"
Chris said. "He wouldn't sit up at
the table and he spilled his milk.
He made a terrible fuss."

"That's too bad,"
said Chris's father.

"When we went to the park Alexander wouldn't play with the others. He got scared and ran and hid behind the slide. Mommy said she was surprised at a big grown-up horse acting like that."

"I'll bet you were, too," Chris's father said.

"Well, sort of," said Chris.

"What else happened?" Chris's father asked.

"Well, we went to the grocery store. And Alexander swished his tail and knocked over a jar of peaches by accident—and broke it."

"I guess it's pretty hard for a horse in a grocery store," Chris's father said.

"He'd better be more careful," Chris said, "or we won't be able to take him shopping with us any more."

"That wouldn't be much fun," his father said.

"Did Alexander take his nap?" Chris's father asked.

"He says horses don't take naps. They just sit on their beds and play with their toys."

"Don't they get awfully tired?"

"And cross, too," Chris nodded. "Alexander was cross all afternoon."

"Why, what did he do?" asked Chris's father.

"Well," Chris said . . .

"He wouldn't tie his shoelaces...

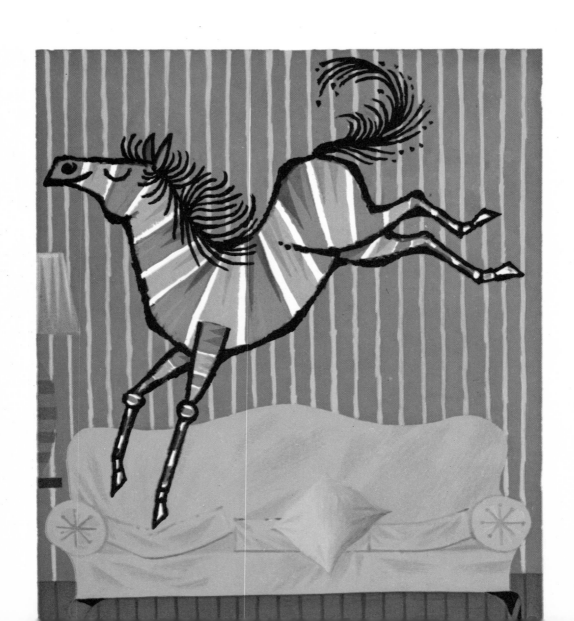

"And he jumped
and jumped
all over the living-room couch
even when Mommy asked him
not to . . .

"And he got angry and kicked my little fire engine and broke the wheel off it..."

"Oh-oh!" said Chris's father.

"And he splashed water all over the bathroom when he had his bath . . .

"And he wouldn't brush his teeth . . .

"Or pick up his toys . . ."

"Whew! What a cross horse!" Chris's father said.

Chris moved closer and leaned his head against his father's arm. "Daddy, what are we going to do about Alexander? He's awfully bad sometimes."

His father was looking at the toy fire engine and the
wheel that had come off it. "What do *you* think we ought
to do?"

Chris thought a moment. "Well," he said . . .

"Mommy could make a jail under the dining-room table and put him there when he's terrible."

Chris's father shook his head. "Mommy wouldn't ever do that," he said.

"Or maybe you could tie him up to the bed and not let him go for ten whole days."

But Chris's father shook his head again. "No sir!" he said. "Not me!"

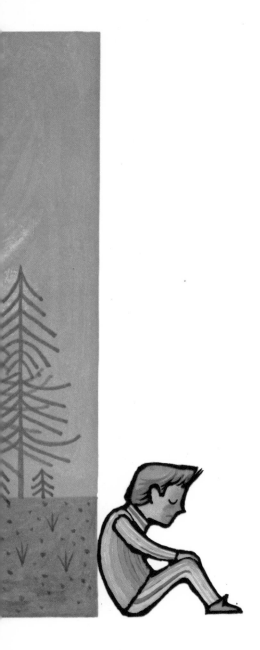

"Maybe I should tell him to go away and never come back again as long as he lives," Chris said doubtfully.

"I'd miss him," his father said.

Chris put his elbows on his knees and rested his chin in his hands. "Then what *are* we going to do about that old Alexander?" he asked.

His father stood up. "I'm going to think about that while I fix this fire engine," he said.

Chris's father went out to the kitchen. He took the hammer from the shelf over the broom closet and a nail from the coffee can under the sink. He set the toy engine down on a kitchen chair, held the wheel in place, and hammered the engine and the wheel back together again.

He spun the wheel around a few times to see that it worked perfectly. Then he put the hammer back on the shelf above the broom closet and went back to Chris.

"Did you think about Alexander?" Chris asked, trying out the little fire engine on his bed.

"I thought and thought," his father said.

"What did you decide?" asked Chris.

His father put the fire engine in Chris's toy box for the night.

"I decided he just had a bad day."

He helped Chris wriggle down in bed and handed him his big brown bear.

"And I think anybody can have a bad day once in a while—even a red horse with green stripes."

He tucked the covers in and kissed Chris on the nose.

"You wait," he said. "Alexander will be a wonderful little horse tomorrow."

He turned out the bedroom light.

"And you'll be a wonderful little boy, too."

Chris giggled. "How did you know I wasn't very nice
today?" he asked.